A NOTE TO PARENTS

When your children are ready to "step into reading," giving them the right books is as crucial as giving them the right food to eat. **Step into Reading Books** present exciting stories and information reinforced with lively, colorful illustrations that make learning to read fun, satisfying, and worthwhile. They are priced so that acquiring an entire library of them is affordable. And they are beginning readers with a difference—they're written on five levels.

Early Step into Reading Books are designed for brand-new readers, with large type and only one or two lines of very simple text per page. **Step 1 Books** feature the same easy-to-read type as the Early Step into Reading Books, but with more words per page. **Step 2 Books** are both longer and slightly more difficult, while **Step 3 Books** introduce readers to paragraphs and fully developed plot lines. **Step 4 Books** offer exciting nonfiction for the increasingly independent reader.

The grade levels assigned to the five steps—preschool through kindergarten for the Early Books, preschool through grade 1 for Step 1, grades 1 through 3 for Step 2, grades 2 through 3 for Step 3, and grades 2 through 4 for Step 4—are intended only as guides. Some children move through all five steps very rapidly; others climb the steps over a period of several years. Either way, these books will help your child "step into reading" in style!

With love to
William Carson Shefelman,
our first grandson:
May this book start you
on the reading trail.

http://www.randomhouse.com

Library of Congress Cataloging-in-Publication Data:
Shefelman, Janice Jordan. Young Wolf and Spirit Horse / by Janice Shefelman
illustrated by Tom Shefelman. p. cm. — (Step into reading. A step 3 book)
SUMMARY: Young Wolf goes in search of his horse Red Wind, which has been spirited away
by a legendary wild stallion.
ISBN 0-679-88207-3 (pbk.) – ISBN 0-679-98207-8 (lib. bdg.)
1. Indians of North America—Juvenile Fiction.
[1. Indians of North America—Fiction. 2. Horses—Fiction.]
I. Shefelman, Tom, ill. II. Title. III. Series: Step into reading. Step 3 book.
PZ7.S54115Ym 1997 [Fic]—dc20 96-25563

Printed in the United States of America 10 9 8 7 6 5 4 3 2 1

STEP INTO READING is a registered trademark of Random House, Inc.

Step into Reading®

Young Wolf
and
Spirit Horse

By Janice Shefelman
Illustrated by Tom Shefelman

A Step 3 Book
Random House 🏠 New York

1
Night Visitor

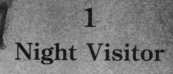

Young Wolf did not want anyone to steal his horse, Red Wind. So every night he tied her rope to his wrist.

"You are my best friend," he told the mare. "You are the smartest, most beautiful horse in the village. And you understand me."

Red Wind turned her ears to catch his words.

"If the Apaches come," he said, "tug on your rope."

Nnnnn-hhhhh, Red Wind answered.

Young Wolf knew that meant *yes.*

Young Wolf crawled
inside the tepee and into
his soft bed.

"Good night," said
Voice of the Sunrise.

"Good night, Mother."

Soon Young Wolf
fell asleep.

He did not hear Spirit Horse
come and chew the rope in two. He
did not wake up when Spirit Horse and
Red Wind galloped away.

At first light Young Wolf opened his eyes. He tugged on Red Wind's rope. Something was wrong—the rope was loose.

He rushed outside. Red Wind was gone!
Young Wolf looked for her hoofprints.
There they were—leading to the meadow.
He knew they were Red Wind's, because
one hoof was chipped.

But there was another set of hoofprints
beside hers.

9

Young Wolf followed the hoofprints across the meadow. The trail ended at a rocky slope.

"Red Wind!" Young Wolf called.

She did not answer.

Young Wolf climbed the slope. Ahead he saw crushed blades of grass.

"The trail!" he shouted.

Young Wolf followed it past Lone Hill, to Lone Hill Creek. There the trail disappeared again.

"Red Wind!" he called. "Red Wind!"

The only answer was the wind in the trees.

Young Wolf turned back to the village. He needed to talk to his father.

"Do you think the Apaches stole her?" Young Wolf asked his father.

"No," said Eagle Feather. He showed the end of the rope to Young Wolf. "See how ragged the rope is? A wild stallion chewed it in two and took Red Wind."

Young Wolf saw. "Will she come back?" he asked.

Eagle Feather shook his head. "A wild stallion keeps his mares for himself."

"Then I will go and get her," said Young Wolf.

"No, my son. Not even a man can take a mare from a wild stallion."

Young Wolf said nothing. His mind was made up. He was going after Red Wind—no matter what Father said.

Young Wolf went to find his friend
Little Big Mouth.

"A wild stallion stole Red Wind last
night," Young Wolf told him.

"Oh, no!" Little Big Mouth said.

Young Wolf moved closer so no one
could hear. "I am going after her."

"And I am going with you," answered
Little Big Mouth.

"You are not afraid of wild stallions?"
Young Wolf asked.

"Nothing scares *me*, Young Wolf."

They both laughed.

Young Wolf knew Little Big Mouth
was bragging. He talked that way to make
himself feel brave.

"Good," said Young Wolf. "Meet me at
the big oak tree before first light."

2

The Search

Early the next morning Young Wolf
waited under the tree. He thought about
the wild stallion.

Once, he had seen two stallions fight
over a mare. They had reared and kicked
and bitten each other. What would a
stallion do to a boy?

Young Wolf shivered in the cool air. If
only Little Big Mouth would come. His talk
made Young Wolf feel brave, too.

Finally he saw Little Big Mouth on his
horse, Shadow, coming across the meadow.

"I had to wait until my father went
back to sleep," he whispered. "He thought
someone was trying to steal Shadow."

Young Wolf got up behind his friend.

"Head for Lone Hill Creek," he said.
"That is where I lost the trail."

The sky had grown light by the time they reached the creek.

"Maybe the stallion led Red Wind through the water," Young Wolf said. "To hide the trail."

"Maybe so," said Little Big Mouth.

"You look upstream," Young Wolf said. "And I'll look downstream."

The two boys searched the banks of the creek for hoofprints.

"I found some!" called Little Big Mouth.

Young Wolf ran to his friend. In the mud were hoofprints.

"Yes! They are hers." Young Wolf knelt and pointed at one of them. "See the chip here? This is Red Wind's left front hoofprint."

All morning they followed the trail. It led them across creeks and past clumps of oak trees.

They climbed a high hill and looked around. But Red Wind and the stallion were nowhere in sight.

The two boys went on following
the trail.

In the afternoon dark clouds slowly
covered the sun. Then thunder rumbled.

Suddenly there was a flash of light
and ...CRACK!

Shadow bolted. Young Wolf held onto
his friend. And Little Big Mouth held onto
Shadow.

On and on the horse galloped, through
the driving rain.

At last they ran out of the storm. Shadow slowed to a stop.

In the valley below, a herd of horses grazed peacefully. There were brown ones, black ones, spotted ones...and Red Wind! Beside her stood a pure white stallion with black ears.

Young Wolf's eyes grew big. Only one stallion looked like that.

"Spirit Horse!" Little Big Mouth whispered.

There were many stories told about Spirit Horse. He had magic powers. No horse in the world could match his strength and speed.

How can I get Red Wind back from him? wondered Young Wolf.

Spirit Horse sniffed the air. He looked up at the boys.

Red Wind raised her head and turned her ears toward them.

"Red Wind!" Young Wolf called.

Spirit Horse reared up. *NNNNNNN-hhhhh!* he screamed.

His mares bolted. Spirit Horse drove
them across the valley—all but Red Wind.
She stood looking at Young Wolf.

"Now is our chance," he said.

Little Big Mouth leaned forward.
Shadow made his way down to the valley.

3
The Fight

Red Wind trotted toward Shadow.
Young Wolf dismounted. He put
his arms around the mare's neck.

"Will you come home with me?"
he whispered in her ear.

Suddenly Red Wind's head went up.

She looked across the valley.

Spirit Horse was galloping toward them.

Young Wolf could not think what to do.

Spirit Horse charged at Shadow.

Shadow reared.

Little Big Mouth fell to the ground.

The two horses met on their hind legs.
Shadow struck at the white stallion with
his hooves. But Spirit Horse got his teeth
on Shadow's neck. Shadow staggered.

Spirit Horse whirled around and
kicked. Shadow went down.

Little Big Mouth ran to his horse
with a cry.

Spirit Horse reared over them.
NNNNNNN-hhhhh! he screamed.

"No!" shouted Young Wolf.

He ran to the white stallion and raised his arms.

"O Spirit Horse," he said. "I send my voice to you. Spare Little Big Mouth and Shadow. They do not want Red Wind."

Spirit Horse tossed his head and pawed the air.

"It is I, Young Wolf, who loves her."

Spirit Horse's pale eyes looked at him.

Then Young Wolf heard a voice like distant thunder.

I will spare your friends, Young Wolf, said the voice. *But Red Wind is mine now. She is happy to be with the horse nation.*

Red Wind trotted to Young Wolf and stood beside him.

Spirit Horse came down on his front legs.

Young Wolf looked at Red Wind. Tears filled his eyes.

"Will I ever see you again?" he asked.

Nnnnn-hhhhh, she said.

"I hope that means yes," Young Wolf said. He stroked the white blaze on her forehead.

Red Wind nuzzled his cheek.

Then she turned to Spirit Horse.
Young Wolf watched as they galloped
off together.

4
Words of Stone

Little Big Mouth washed the bite on Shadow's neck.

"It was a brave thing you did," he said to Young Wolf. "Spirit Horse would have killed us."

Little Big Mouth pressed fresh grass to Shadow's neck.

The sun set, and the moon of blooming meadows rose.

"I don't know the way home," said Young Wolf. "Do you?"

"No," said Little Big Mouth. "But Shadow can show us. All horses know."

"I hope so," said Young Wolf.

Poor-will, poor-will, came the call of a night bird. It was a lonely sound. But not as lonely as Young Wolf felt without Red Wind.

The moon was high when they came to
the village. All the tepees were dark except
two.

"Our mothers keep the fires burning,"
Little Big Mouth said.

"Yes," Young Wolf answered.

"Maybe Red Wind will come back,"
said Little Big Mouth.

"Maybe." Young Wolf turned and
walked to his tepee.

Eagle Feather came out. "You caused us much worry," he said.

"I am sorry, Father. But I had to find Red Wind."

"Come inside," Eagle Feather said. "Your mother and grandfather are waiting."

"Tell us what happened, my son," said Voice of the Sunrise.

Young Wolf told his story. When he finished, no one spoke.

Then Eagle Feather said, "It was not a wise thing that you did. But it *was* brave."

"I only wish Red Wind had come back with me," Young Wolf said.

"Red Wind will always be in your heart," said Grandfather He-Bear. "And someday you will love another horse."

Young Wolf looked down and shook his head. "No, Grandfather, never. I will wait for Red Wind to come back."

Eagle Feather put his hand on Young Wolf's shoulder. "Red Wind is not coming back, my son. She loves Spirit Horse."

The words fell like stones on Young Wolf's heart.

5
Snow Wind

One winter passed, and another came.

Young Wolf grew tall and strong. He had a new horse now. Still, he waited for Red Wind to return.

A heavy snow fell. Young Wolf and Little Big Mouth walked to the meadow.

"Look, there is enough snow to make a Spirit Horse," said Young Wolf. "Then I can send my voice to him."

The two boys worked all morning.
They shaped the horse's head and neck.
They carved his legs and sweeping tail.
They gave him pieces of bark for ears and
round stones for eyes.

Young Wolf raised his arms.

"O Spirit Horse,
You have ears to hear
And eyes to see.
Will Red Wind ever
Come back to me?"

That night Young Wolf dreamed about
Spirit Horse. When he awoke, it was still
dark. He put on his moccasins and
wrapped a buffalo robe around his
shoulders.

Outside the snow had stopped falling.

Young Wolf walked to the snow horse in the meadow.

Everything seemed to be waiting. So Young Wolf waited, too.

Nnnnn-hhhhh.

It was a voice Young Wolf knew well.

Red Wind stood on the top of the rocky slope. Beside her was a colt as white as new snow.

"Red Wind!" whispered Young Wolf. "Have you come back to me?"

But Red Wind did not answer. She just pushed the colt with her nose. He made his way down the slope—alone.

"You are giving me your colt?" asked Young Wolf.

Nnnnn-hhhhh, said Red Wind.

The colt came toward Young Wolf.

"Thank you, Red Wind," he said. His heart filled with joy.

Red Wind gazed at Young Wolf and the colt. Then she turned and galloped away.

The colt stood before him.

"I will call you Snow Wind," said
Young Wolf. He blew his breath into the
colt's nostrils. "Smell who I am."

Snow Wind flared his nostrils. He
turned his black ears to listen.

Just like his mother.